RAVEN
Brings the LIGHT

*Many people know **Gwaii Haanas** on the*

north coast of British Columbia as the Queen

Charlotte Islands. However, for centuries before

Europeans came to this land, these islands were

known to the Haida people who lived there as

***Gwaii Haanas**, the Beautiful Islands. Today,*

*they are officially known as **Haida Gwaii**,*

which means the islands of the Haida.

This book is dedicated to all of the storytellers

from Gwaii Haanas and the northwest

coast who have passed this story down from

generation to generation, all the way back to

when light first came to the world.

Illustrations copyright © 2013 Roy Henry Vickers
Text copyright © 2013 Roy Henry Vickers and Robert Budd

1 2 3 4 5 — 17 16 15 14 13

Harbour Publishing Co. Ltd.
P.O. Box 219, Madeira Park, BC, V0N 2H0
www.harbourpublishing.com

Design by Anna Comfort O'Keeffe
Printed and bound in China

Harbour Publishing acknowledges financial support from the Government of Canada through the Canada Book Fund and the Canada Council for the Arts, and from the Province of British Columbia through the BC Arts Council and the Book Publishing Tax Credit.

Library and Archives Canada Cataloguing in Publication

Vickers, Roy Henry, 1946-
     Raven brings the light / Roy Henry Vickers and Robert Budd ; illustrated by Roy Henry Vickers.

ISBN 978-1-55017-593-6

     1. Tsimshian Indians—British Columbia—Folklore—Juvenile literature. 2. Raven (Legendary character)—Juvenile literature. 3. Legends—British Columbia—Juvenile literature. 4. British Columbia—Folklore—Juvenile literature. I. Budd, Robert, 1976- II. Title.

E99.T8V52 2013   j398.209711'1   C2013-900010-0

ROY HENRY VICKERS *and* ROBERT BUDD

Illustrated by ROY HENRY VICKERS

RAVEN
Brings the LIGHT

HARBOUR
PUBLISHING

M ANY YEARS AGO THE WORLD LIVED IN DARKNESS.

In this darkness a young couple on Gwaii Haanas became parents to a baby boy. It did not take them long to realize there was something very different and very special about their son. They called him Weget.

We means big. *Get* means man. *Weget* means big man.

This boy got the name Weget because he was growing so fast that it frightened his mother and father.

They brought him to the old people and said, "Something is wrong with our child, Weget. We don't know what's wrong. He is just a baby, yet he's already walking. How can this be possible?"

The Elders took one look at the child and they nodded their heads and they smiled.

They told the parents, "For many years we have been told that this child was coming to be with us. We will get all the Chiefs together and you will learn what this child will be."

And so the Chiefs got together to meet with this couple. They brought a big treasure chest made of cedar, known as a *guloonich*.

The Chiefs told the parents, "Our leaders have known for generations that one day a boy would come to this place, a boy who would change the whole world. This child may have been born to you, but he belongs to everybody. Right now we live in darkness. This boy is going to bring the light. We have some things passed down from generation to generation in this guloonich to give to this boy."

Out of the box they pulled a magic raven skin made from the feathers, beak and claws of a real raven, but much, much larger than any normal raven.

They explained, "When Weget grows big enough, he can put on this raven skin. When he wears it, he will be able to fly. He will also be able to change himself into anything he wants."

The Chiefs continued, "Our people have been told that one day Weget is going to leave our island, and he is going to fly over the big waters to get the Daylight Ball from the Chief of the Heavens and bring it back to us."

Then they reached into the box and pulled out a little skin pouch. They opened it up and it was full of little rocks.

"When Weget flies over the big water, he will get tired. He should take one of these rocks and drop it in the big ocean. The little rock will change into an island where he can land and rest."

"After Weget passes over the water, he will come to a big land where there are no islands."

The Chiefs reached into the box and pulled out another little skin pouch. They opened the pouch up carefully and revealed little red fish eggs. After closing it, they put it back in the box and continued, "When Weget comes to the big land, there will be waters running off of the land into the salt water. When he gets to the place where the waters meet, he will take these eggs and put them into the moving water. And he is to say, 'Let all of these rivers bring forth an abundance of fish for my people.'"

The Chiefs took out one more bag. And in that bag was a variety of berry and tree seeds.

"When Weget gets to the big land, he is to spread these seeds all over the land. And these seeds are going to bring all kinds of trees and foods to our people."

Weget continued to grow and the time soon came when he was ready to receive his gifts. As he slipped on the raven skin for the first time his heart was filled with courage. The Chiefs had prepared him as well as they could.

With great excitement he tucked the cedar box underneath his arm and took flight. Before long, however, Weget began to lose his way in the darkness. He became so tired flying back and forth, he was forced to drop many rocks in order to rest. Today, there are many islands along the West Coast—these are the rocks Weget dropped in the water.

Weget finally arrived at the big land and he saw a mighty river coming down.

The river is known today as the Skeena, but in the old times it was called *Ksien* and so the people who live around it are called the *Gitksien*, which means "people of Ksien." As Weget flew northward over the land he remembered to drop the fish eggs into the rivers, and spread the seeds all over the land.

After Weget flew over Ksien he came to *Lisims*, known today as the Nass River. The Chiefs had told Weget that this river would rise very quickly up into the mountains.

Up there, the river turned into a creek, which turned into a small rivulet, before it came to the place where the juice from the clouds fell on the mountain.

When Weget reached this place he was told to look straight up into the sky where he would see a little wee light … *waaaaay* up there. That was where he was to go.

As he flew higher he discovered that the pinpoint of light was actually a big hole in the sky, a hole in the heavens.

Up there, there was light.

Upon entering the hole in the sky, Weget was afraid because everything was strange and bright. He had lived all his life in darkness and did not know what light was. It hurt his eyes but he was excited to see everything so clearly. He could see a village in the distance with smoke coming from the houses. He could see the enormous longhouse where the Chief of the Heavens kept the Daylight Ball.

The Chief kept the Daylight Ball in a bent box. Weget knew he must go to the Chief and ask for the Daylight Ball so he could take it back to light the world.

He took off his raven skin and left it right beside the hole, and he started walking up to the Chief of the Heavens' house. There were two men standing by the door and they stopped him.

Weget said, "My name is Weget and I come from the darkness down below. All my people live in darkness. I have come to the Chief of the Heavens because he has the Daylight Ball and I must bring that ball back to my people down below."

And so they let him in.

Weget walked up to the Chief of the Heavens and explained who he was, where he came from, and the difficulty his people had living all their lives in darkness. He told the Chief of the Heavens about everything he had done on his journey, and that getting the Daylight Ball was his last task.

The Chief of the Heavens looked at Weget and said, "You cannot have the Daylight Ball."

Weget thought to himself, "This isn't supposed to happen. I'm supposed to get the Daylight Ball and take it to my people. What am I going to do now?"

Weget left the longhouse and began to walk back to the hole in the sky. All he wanted was to put his raven skin back on and leave, because he felt defeated. But then he remembered he had some tricks.

He saw a cedar tree by a little creek, not far from the house. He put on the raven skin and flew up into the branches.

Weget sat patiently and looked around, watching everything.

Eventually a beautiful young woman walked out of the Chief of the Heavens' longhouse. She was the Chief's daughter. She came down to the creek carrying a waterproof cedar box. It was a really hot day, and she was getting water for the house.

She dipped a ladle into the water and began to fill the box. After a few dips she looked around and thought to herself, "Is there anyone around? I know my father said I'm not supposed to drink the water until it's blessed, but I'm so thirsty."

She looked around again.

Then she took a sip, *slrrrp.*

Once again she looked around to make sure she was not seen. Then she took the box back to the longhouse.

But Weget was watching. "Ahhh! She's a tricky one. She's just like the kids back home, doing things they are not supposed to do when nobody is watching. Now I know how I'm going to get the Chief's Daylight Ball."

The next time the young woman came, Weget flew up the creek and took the raven skin off. He hid it underneath some bushes, grabbed a leaf and studied it. Then he changed himself into a leaf and floated down the river and right into the young woman's dipper.

The young woman spotted the leaf in her dipper and threw the leaf back in the water before drinking.

Weget, the little leaf, floated away thinking, "Oh, that didn't work. I've got to figure out a better way."

He flew into a fir tree and began to think. Weget noticed that the branch of the tree did not have any leaves. Instead, fir trees have very soft, tiny little needles.

So along came Weget, as a tiny little needle, floating down the river. He floated right into the young woman's dipper. Once again she looked around and took a sip, *slrrrp*, swallowing Weget whole!

Soon after the Chief's daughter gave birth to a beautiful baby boy, never suspecting it was really tricky little Weget.

The Chief of the Heavens loved his new grandson and did everything he could to make him happy.

The baby would scream "Waaaaaah!" while pointing at the box that contained the Daylight Ball.

Grandpa would lovingly take down the box, open the lid and give the baby the Daylight Ball to play with. Baby Weget was happy, playing around with the Daylight Ball at his grandpa's house.

As he would play, he would inch his way closer to the door. Grandpa would scold, "That's enough, grandson!" Then Grandpa would take the Daylight Ball and put it back in the box.

This happened every day. Weget would cry until he got the ball, then he would play with it.

After a while, Grandpa got so used to the baby playing with the Daylight Ball that he stopped watching him. One day when Weget was playing by the front door, he took the Daylight Ball and ran as fast as he could.

He didn't even look back.

He raced straight to the hole in the sky. Upon arriving, he put the Daylight Ball in the bent box and put the lid on. He quickly slipped the raven skin on and *whoosh*, he landed back on the banks of the Lisims.

Weget was tired and hungry.

As Weget's belly rumbled, he noticed some frog spirits fishing in the dark. They had already caught lots of fish. He called to them, "Oh, my brothers, I would like a fish. I'm so hungry. I've been working really hard."

And the frog spirits said, "Beat it Weget. Leave us alone. Get your own fish."

Weget thought, "That's not very nice of them. I put those fish in that river." So he tried again, "My brothers. You are really good fishermen. All I would like is one fish."

The frogs taunted, "Beat it Weget. Leave us alone! Get your own fish. We are busy here, you can see."

Weget began to get angry. A third time he spoke, "My brothers. I put those fish in that river. You shouldn't be so greedy. Just give me one fish, that's all I want."

But the frogs answered, "Leave us alone Weget, beat it. We are tired of you asking us."

Weget offered the frog spirits a last chance: "Alright. My brothers, I want a fish. I'm hungry. I put those fish in that river. You can get lots of fish. If you don't give me a fish, I'm going to open this box and let out a big, bright light and you will disappear. You will never be able to fish again. I just want one fish."

The frogs replied, "Beat it Weget, you liar. We know how tricky you are."

Upon hearing these words, Weget took the top off the box.

Whoooosh.

The Sun flew up into the sky where it brought light to the whole world. The world cast off its darkness, all the beautiful colours came out and it was hot.

A wind started to blow. It came down the river, to the ocean, and the frogs were blown to the mouth of the Lisims where they turned to stone.

The people on the West Coast are known as the Salmon People. Weget's efforts brought all the different kinds of salmon to our waters and our tables. Our people have been able to fish and pick berries now for thousands of years.

The fireweed that grows on the mountainsides is the first vegetable that comes to our people each spring. Before the salmonberries come, their little shoots grow every year and they are very soft. We peel the skin off them, and eat the shoots. We eat strawberries, blueberries, blackberries and so many others.

All these foods come from the seeds that were spread all over the world by Weget. They grow from the heat of the sun that clever Weget put in the sky.

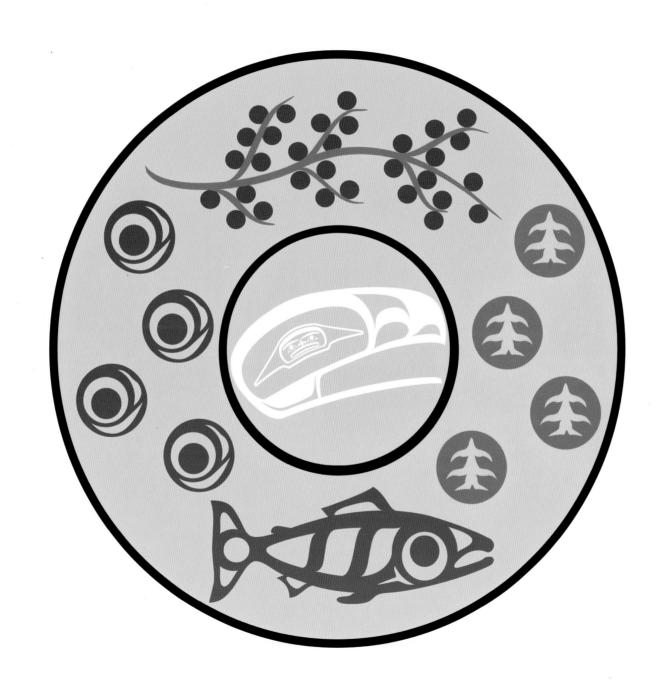

The story in this book belongs to the people of the northwest coast. It has been passed from generation to generation for thousands of years. It's my great joy to share it with you, as it was told to me by Chester Bolton, Chief of the Ravens, from the village of Kitkatla around 1975.

   —Roy Henry Vickers